W9-BGN-485

FREE PUBLIC LIBRARY
UXBRIDGE, MA 01569

jj
Ziefert

for my friend Nemo
—T.M.

Published by Sterling Publishing Co., Inc.
387 Park Avenue South, New York, NY 10016

Text © 2004 by Harriet Ziefert
Illustrations © 2004 by Todd McKie

Distributed in Canada by Sterling Publishing
c/o Canadian Manda Group, One Atlantic Avenue, Suite 105
Toronto, Ontario, Canada M6K 3E7
Distributed in Great Britain by Chrysalis Books
64 Brewery Road, London N79NT, England
Distributed in Australia by Capricorn Link (Australia) Pty. Ltd.
P.O. Box 704, Windsor, NSW 2756, Australia

All rights reserved. No part of this publication may be reproduced, stored in a retrieval
system, or transmitted, in any form or by any means, electronic, mechanical, photocopying,
recording, or otherwise, without prior written permission from the publisher.

ISBN 1-4027-1617-6

Color separations by Bright Arts
Printed in China
All rights reserved

10   9   8   7   6   5   4   3   2   1

September, 2004

Harriet Ziefert

44 Uses for a Dog

drawings by Todd McKie

Sterling Publishing Co., Inc.

New York

1.

anti-depressant

2.

nanny

3.

trailblazer

4.
alarm clock

5.

lumberjack

6.
pet sitter

7.

footstool

8.

letter carrier

9.

smoke detector

10.

washcloth

11.
copilot

12.

housekeeper

13.

yoga instructor

14.
athletic director

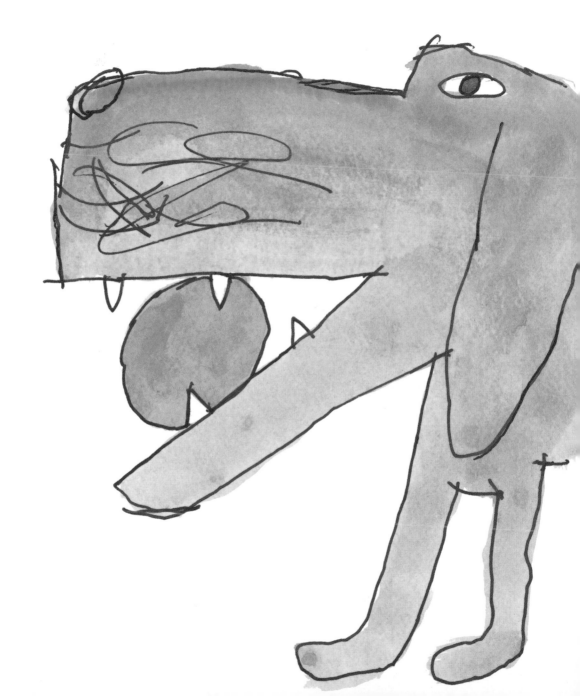

15.

matchmaker

16.

lawn sprinkler

17.

garbage disposal

18.
Food critic

19.
confidante

20.
pest control

21.
dinner companion

22.
friend

23.

audience

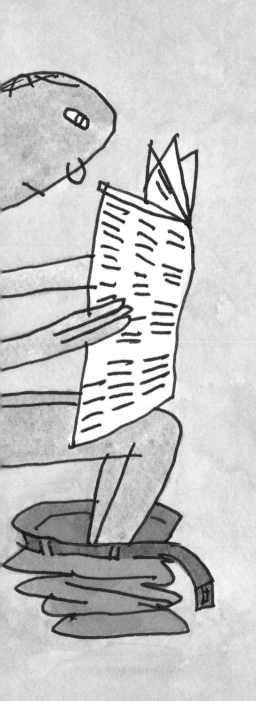

24.
gardener

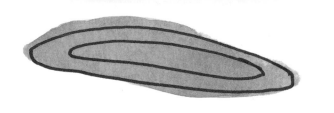

25.
air traffic controller

26.

bearer of gifts

27.

bone specialist

28.

personal trainer

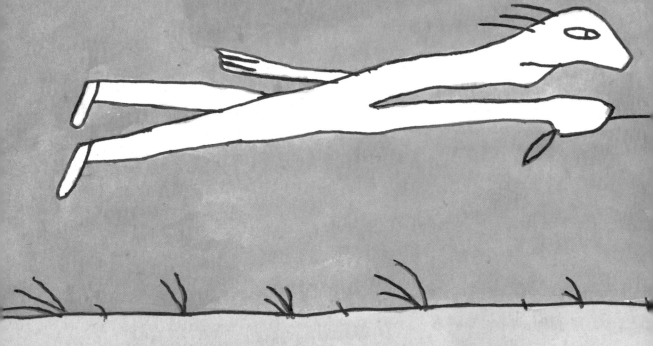

29.
therapist

30.

vacuum cleaner

31.
dishwasher

32.

guard

33.

pillow

34.

meat inspector

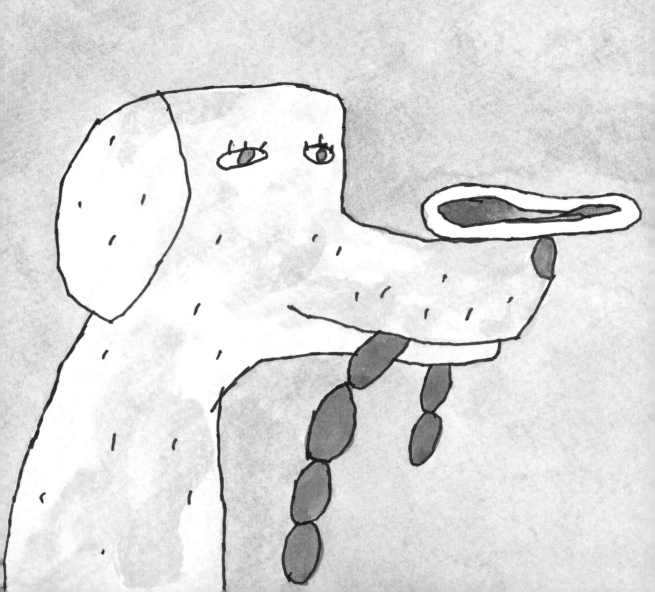

35.
party animal

36.
swim buddy

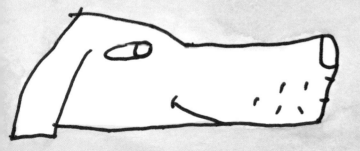

37.
travel
companion

38.
lawn fertilizer

39.
weight trainer

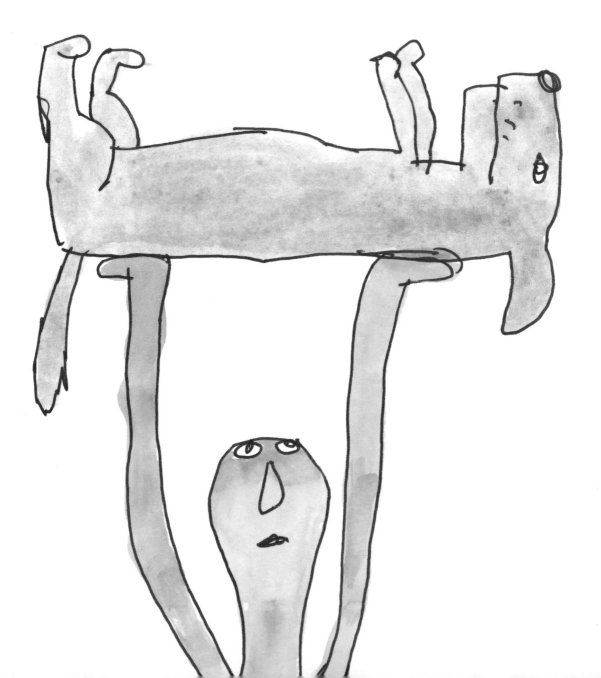

40.
dance partner

41.

landscape architect

42.
accomplice

43.

zen master

44.

family

37393000439824

jj   Ziefert, Harriet.
            44 uses for a dog.

FREE PUBLIC LIBRARY
UXBRIDGE, MA 01569

GAYLORD M